© N. W. DAMM & SØN AS

N-0055 Oslo

Tel: +47 24 05 10 00

9. printing

Design: Skomsøy Grønli AS

Translations: Berlitz GlobalNET

Printed in Denmark by Nørhaven Book

N·W·DAMM&SØN

# The Little Troll

by
Tor Åge Bringsværd

illustrations by
Ingerlise Karlsen Kongsgaard

There have always been trolls here in the north. Long before human beings lived here, trolls lived in the forests and mountains.

Some have three heads, others have two, but most of them have only one.

Many people are afraid of trolls. They believe that trolls are bad. But trolls are just like people. Some are good and some are bad. Some are wise and some are.......not so smart.

We hardly ever see trolls because they prefer to be left in peace. As far as they are concerned, people and their machines are terribly noisy. That´s why they hide whenever anyone approaches. They sit very still trying to look like old tree stumps or moss-covered rocks.

But they are friends with all birds and animals. They always help any animal that is sick or injured. Whenever a baby animal gets lost, trolls can be out all night long looking for it. And if there is too little food, they cheerfully invite the bears, moose and foxes home to eat with them.

They cook up a big pot of troll porridge.

Troll porridge is all they ever eat. For that reason it is also their absolute favorite.

Trolls like the forests and meadows to look nice. They take care of the flowers and trees and try to keep things as tidy as they can. But it´s not an easy job!

This is a story about a troll child named Little Troll.

"Little Troll!" calls Mama. "Come on home now! It will soon be light!"

"Just a little longer, Mama! says Little Troll. "We´re having such a good time!"

"No," says Mama. "Come at once! It´s almost morning! And you know what that means!"

Trolls, you see, are afraid of the sun.

Little Troll and his parents live inside a mountain. They have a secret entrance behind a large boulder by a hazel thicket.

First Little Troll eats a bowl of troll porridge. Then he brushes his teeth with a pine twig. And then... he finally goes to bed in his pine cone bed.

Mama sits beside him for a while as she always does. She sings to him for a little while. Then they talk about the things they´ve seen and done that night.

But this time all Little Troll wants to talk about is the sun. "Why is it so? Why must we hide from it?"

"Some say we will crumble and turn to stone if the sun shines on us. Others say that we will melt and turn into nothing."

"That´s not fair!"

"But that is the way it is - and that is the way it has always been. And now you must go to sleep," says Mama as she tucks his blanket of bark snuggly around him.

But Little Troll doesn´t want to go to sleep.

He calls out to his papa. "Why is it so, Papa? Why can´t we trolls be out in the sun like everyone else?"

But Papa just shakes his big shaggy head. "I don´t know," he says. "But that is the way it is - and that is the way it has always been. And if you don´t go to sleep soon, you´ll be too tired to do anything tonight."

But Little Troll can´t sleep.

He keeps thinking about the sun. That big, hot and treacherous light in the sky.

Quietly he sneaks over to a little crack in the mountain wall and peeks out.

It´s so beautiful out there! Everything is so much more vivid than at night! Colors are brighter and very beautiful. And he can see animals running around playing. Little Troll would so much like to play with them too. But he cannot. Because he might melt like a snowball - or explode into a thousand pieces. It´s not fair!

He thinks of all the scarey stories he has heard about trolls who were careless and didn´t make it home in time - or who got tricked by bad human boys out on adventures...

He remembers the big pile of rocks down the mountain side. "That´s all that is left of our forefather," says Mama each time they pass it. She always points out what is supposed to have been his nose and perhaps a hand...

Jumping junipers, it´s so unfair!"

The next evening Little Troll gets up early and is out the door as soon as the sun has set. He hardly even takes time to tie the bow on his tail. For he has decided that he wants an answer! There must be someone out there who can tell him more?

"Do you want to play? asks the moose calf.

"Don´t have time," says Little Troll.

"I´ll come along anyway," says the moose calf.

First they run down to the waterfall.

Uncle Rustibust lives there under the rotting old bridge.

Uncle Rustibust just loves to tease anybody who crosses his bridge. He pretends to be angry and dangerous. "Who´s that tramping on my bridge?" he bellows.

Everyone knows it´s just a game and that Uncle Rustibust thinks it´s great fun when you pretend to be afraid.

But once, long ago, there came three billy goats who didn´t know the game. They took it all very seriously. It ended with them butting Uncle Rustibust out into the waterfall before they continued on their way up the mountain to some hut. Poor Uncle Rustibust - who couldn´t even swim!

Ever since that day, he never tries to tease billy goats. All you have to do is say "baaaa" and he gets very quiet....

But Uncle Rustibust is no help to Little Troll either. "Why can´t we go out in daylight?" he says, scratching his furry ears. "I guess that´s just the way it is..."

But Little Troll wants a better answer than that. So he goes to see someone even older. He goes to see the silly sisters on Gray Ridge - Trollie and Trolla.

Neither of the sisters have eyes in their heads. They do however have one big one they can hold in their hands, which they are very afraid of dropping on the floor since it would be so awfully hard to find. Because they only have the one eye between them, they must walk very close together, holding each other's tail. They take turns going first, of course.

"No," say the two silly sisters. "We can't help you. That's the way it's been since long before our time, and we're over three hundred years old each. That makes about six hundred years altogether!"

"But who can I ask then?" cries Little Troll. "Surely no one is older than that?"

"Talk to Arnulf," say the silly sisters. "He lives just beyond the next mountain, and he's much older than us."

"Want to play?" asks the little bear cub.

"Don't have time," says Little Troll. "I'll come along anyway," says the bear cub.

The three friends run through the woods and hills.

Little Troll knows that he must get there before morning. And it is already getting light above the tree tops...

They find Arnulf down by the great cloudberry marsh. He is walking along all bent over with his nose dragging on the ground.

"What are you looking for?" asks Little Troll.

"My heart," says Arnulf. "Who are you?"

Little Troll tells him his name and greets him from the two silly sisters. "But shouldn't we get inside someplace? he asks. "I think the sun is about to rise!"

"Goodness sakes!" exclaims Arnulf. "I completely lost track of time! It's a good thing you came along. Look," he says, lifting a flat rock. "Here is the entrance to my cave. Follow me!"

The moose calf and the bear cub are welcome to join them, but they'd rather wait outside. In the sunshine. It's not fair, says Little Troll to himself, sighing deeply as he crawls down into the darkness. Jumping junipers!

Arnulf explains that his line of trolls comes from a fine family of giants on the west coast. "In our family," he says, "it is tradition not to wear our hearts on us. That way we remain almost invincible. It's almost impossible to do us in, because we never have our hearts about us! We do everything possible to hide them in clever places where thieves won't find them!"

"But now you can't even find it yourself?" asks Little Troll.

"No, that's the thing," says Arnulf. "I've totally forgotten where I hid it! That's just the problem...." Then he sucks in his breath, smiles nervously and would rather talk about something else.

When Little Troll asks him about the sun, Arnulf answers like all the rest. "That's just the way it is - and that's the way it's always been," he says. "But there is a silly old troll who lives on the other side of the Great Lake. Maybe *he* knows more?

14

Little Troll sets out again as soon as it gets dark.

The moose calf and the bear cub have been waiting for him and now a little fox joins them too.

"You are welcome to borrow my boat," Arnulf calls after them. "Just push it off after you land. It will find its way home by itself!"

Behind a pine tree, just beside the railroad tracks, they hear someone singing.

Little Troll stops and listens. It's an odd song. It's a rhyme about princesses. But the words don't really mean anything.

A tall, skinny troll is lying there in the mountain cranberry bushes.

He jumps with a start when Little Troll and his friends appear. "Oh, dear!" he exclaims. "For a moment I almost thought it was a princess!"

"Do I look like a princess then?" says Little Troll.

"No, not exactly. But I can't seem to think about anything but princesses! Say, look out - here comes the night express!"

Everyone drops to the ground and stays perfectly still while the train passes.

"But are there any princesses left these days?" asks Little Troll, once they are all on their feet again. "Didn't they die out ages ago? That's what Papa says anyway..."

"Princesses won't ever die out!" insists the tall, skinny troll. "Who knows, maybe there was one on that train that just passed us. A princess in a white silken gown with a gold crown on her head. Just like the one in my dreams! Just like the one I lie here waiting for."

"But if you want to meet a princess, surely you must go out into the world?" asks Little Troll.

"They didn't have to in the old days," he says. "Because in the old days there were lots of proud and beautiful princesses who also dreamt about us. Who went longing to be enchanted by a real troll. Why can't it still be like that? Why can't she just step down off that train?"

Little Troll has no answer for him.

"Anyway, I´m too shy to go off anywhere," says the other troll. "I get woozy in the head from all the comotion. I know, because I´ve been trying to change. Do you think I´m lying here for fun? Hardly! I´m trying to get used to the hubbub of humans. But it´s not going so well. My head hurts more all the time. Here comes a train from the other direction. Maybe that´s the one she´s on?

Little Troll finally gets a chance to ask his question. But the tall, skinny troll can´t give him a proper answer either. He hardly even tries. All he wants to talk about is princesses. But at least he can tell him where to go, which is to the next troll homestead. "An old troll woman lives there, and she has seen and done just about everything. If she can´t help you, no one can! Must you go already? Can´t we sit awhile and talk about princesses?"

The next troll homestead is impossible to find. For the simple reason that it is invisible. Little Troll and his friends can hear the barnyard dog barking. They can hear the cows lowing in the barn and the horses neighing in their stalls. But they can´t see a thing.

Suddenly a great shadow towers over them. A shadow with three heads.

"Welcome to our farm," says a rusty old voice.

"What do you want here?" asks another voice.

"Get out!" says a third.

But all the while, it´s the same person speaking - a huge old troll woman with three heads. And the three heads clearly don´t agree on anything.

"I wonder if you would help me?" asks Little Troll.

"Of course," replies the first head. "That all depends," says the second head.

"Absolutely not" shouts the third head. "I´m not at all interested in helping you. Not in the least!"

And then the three heads begin to quarrel.

Little Troll sits listening to them for a long time. Jumping junipers! he thinks to himself. It must be awful never being able to agree with yourself!

"Don´t you ever agree on anything?" he finally asks.

"Sure we do!" says the first head. "No!" says the second head.

"I can´t be bothered to speak to any of you!" says the third head, closing her eyes as well as her mouth.

The animals pull at Little Troll to get his attention. "You´ll never get a proper answer here!" they say. "Come on - we should start thinking about heading home. Our parents must be wondering what´s become of us!"

"Climb up on my back," says the moose calf. "Then we can go faster!"

And they run off into the night, by the bright light of the moon.

The animals know a lot of shortcuts.

At one place they stop and rest upon a hilltop. Even though the moose calf is robust, he still needs to rest his legs a little.

The bear cub and the fox gather berries for them to eat. There's also plenty of water to drink in the brook.

But Little Troll is sad. "Perhaps I'll never get an answer," he says sadly. "But jumping junipers, how I hate it when everyone says that something is a certain way just because it is that way!"

"Perhaps I can help?" a crackly old voice suddenly whispers.

None of them can see who is there. "I'm tired of playing the invisible game!" cries Little Troll. "Come out, whoever you are!"

"But I'm not at all invisible," says the voice. "All four of you are sitting right on the middle of my head!"

It's the hill speaking! "Who in the world are you?" asks Little Troll.

"I'm a troll, just like you!," replies the hill. "Walk around me a little. Then maybe you can see me better!"

Little Troll and the three animals walk around the hill. Now that they look carefully, they can see a nose... and two eyes.... and a mouth! He is a troll - a very old one - overgrown with grass and peat and moss. There are even small shrubs growing on him!

"But why are you just sitting here?" wonders Little Troll.

"I'm not sitting," replies the old troll. "I'm walking. I just move so slowly that no one sees me. I've got plenty of time. I'm in no hurry."

"But it doesn't look like you're moving at all."

"That's just because everything else is moving so darn fast these days!"

The sky is getting lighter in the east. Little Troll knows that he must find shelter for the day.

"If you´re afaid of the sun, you can move in close to me," says the old troll. "Crawl in under my moss so you will feel safer."

They are right up next to each other.

"You´ve lived a long time. Why must we trolls always hide from the sun?" asks Little Troll.

"We don´t have to at all," says the old troll. "That´s only something we believe. Look at me!"

"Yes, but you´re all covered with grass and moss and shrubs," says Little Troll. "So it doesn´t count."

"We are Night Children," says the old troll. "Once we were very cold. Once we were Hoarfrost Gnomes and Ice Giants. But that was a long time ago. In the very beginning. Almost before anything else. Because we are the Very Oldest. Never forget that, Little Troll. We were here before any other living creatures. We are older than the forest - indeed, almost as old as the mountains!"

"But why can´t we stand being in the daylight?"

"Because thousands of years ago when Hoarfrost Gnomes wandered here, their hearts were cold as well. Like great clumps of ice inside their breasts.

"And what about today?"

"The old troll laughs. "I don´t think it means a thing these days." His laughter sounds like a squeaky door.

"You´re just teasing me!" cries Little Troll in anger. "Jumping junipers! Everyone knows how dangerous it is to let the sun shine on you!".

"Have you tried though?"

"I´ve seen enough of what happens to those who have! All that is left is a pile of stones!"

"That was back when we fought and ravaged like wild mountain ogres," says the old troll. "When our females rode on wolves and used vipers for reins. But that was long, long ago. In those days, so many trolls were hard and cold-hearted and bad that it was horrible! But anyone who thinks warm thoughts needn´t ever be afraid of anything."

"Nonsense!" Little Troll is so angry that he is about to leave, but it´s too late to find other shelter.

"The only thing dangerous out there is people," says the old troll. "You must watch out for them. But the sun... the sun is nothing to be afraid of."

"That's easy for you to say," grunts Little Troll. "You're not much more than a big clump of moss!" He doesn't want to go to sleep, but he notices that his eyes are beginning to close and that it's harder and harder to stay awake. After all, it is almost the middle of the day.

"You have to take the risk," says the old troll. "You have to dare!"

Little Troll pulls the moss and peat tightly around himself. It has begun to rain.

It rains all day and all night.

Little Troll doesn't wake up until the bear cub comes and jiggles him. "You have to get up now," he says. We're still a long way from home".

The four friends say goodby to the old troll and run on. Through the mud and pouring rain.

There is much hullabaloo when Little Troll returns home. Everyone has been out looking for him. Mama and Papa had nearly given up hope of ever seeing their child again.

First they wrap their arms around him, hugging and kissing him until he can hardly breathe.

And then they begin to scold. What a little scoundrel! they cry. Imagine frightening us all like that!

"You march straight to bed this instant! yells Papa.

"But it's so long ëtil morning, exclaims Little Troll.

"You get into that pine cone bed right now!" replies Mama.

"And you can stay there a whole week!" shouts Papa.

"But I just wanted to... " says Little Troll.

"No just!" cry Mama and Papa in unison.

Towards the middle of the day, there is a terrible storm with thunder and lightening.

Little Troll sits up in his bed with a start. Wasn't that someone calling his name? Someone who needs help?

Mama and Papa are sleeping. They don't hear a thing.

There are the cries again. It's his animal friends!

Little Troll jumps out of bed and runs to the crack in the mountain wall.

But where are they?
If it were nighttime, he could run out and look for them. But he can't. Because now it's daytime. And even though it's raining, it's still light outside!

But now he sees them!

Lightening has struck down a tree.
And the moose calf is caught in its big
branches.

The bear cub and the fox are trying
to pull him loose. But they can´t.
The branches are too heavy. Neither
the fox´s cunning nor the bear´s
strength is enough to free him.
And the moose calf is crying so.

Many other animals are hurrying to help now too. But none of them can budge the toppled tree.

"Just wait until it gets dark!" cries Little Troll. "Then Papa and I will come and help."

The bear cub hears his voice and comes over to the side of the mountain. "That will be too late, Little Troll," he says sadly. "The moose calf can hardly breathe any longer. No one can live very long without breath..."

That's when Little Troll makes his decision. My friend needs help, he thinks to himself. And if I don't do something, he may die! You have to take the risk! You have to dare! That's what the old troll said...

But first Little Troll goes over to the cupboard by the door. That's where Papa keeps the huge, old sword and strength potion that were passed on to him from his grandfather. The sword is so heavy that even Papa must take a gulp before he can swing it around. Which he only does when he wants to show off for guests.

Little Troll takes a big gulp. It tastes awful! But he is almost able to lift the sword down from the wall.

One more big gulp. Jumping junipers, it is terrrible tasting stuff! But suddenly he feels strong enough to swing the sword as if it were a little stick!

Little Troll holds the sword with both hands.

He thinks of the Treacherous Sun. Of how it can make a troll crumble to pieces or melt.

He thinks of the old troll who said it wasn't that treacherous after all.

But most of all he thinks of the moose calf who needs his help.

*You have to take the risk! You have to dare!*

Little Troll swallows deeply. He closes his eyes. And he runs.

Out of the mountain. Out into the Daylight!

"Here I come!" he cries.

All at once it stops raining. The sun breaks through!

Little Troll lifts his arms to protect himself. This is it! he thinks. I´m going to explode!

But nothing happens.

Little Troll rushes across the little green clearing in the woods. The sun is shining. And he is every bit as alive as he was before.

Little Troll swings the sword as if it were an ax. He chops off all the branches that are holding the moose calf captive. Thanks to Papa´s strength potion he has super powers! He grabs the tree trunk with both hands - and lifts it - just enough so the bear cub and the fox can pull the poor moose calf free.

"Hurray!" shout all the animals. "Hurray for Little Troll!"

And they shout so loudly with joy that it wakes even the trolls.

"What´s going on?" grunts a grumpy Papa. "Who is so foolish as to dare wake us in the middle of broad daylight?"

"Good grief, child!" cries Mama. "Have you lost your wits?"

But Little Troll just laughs and beckons to them. "Come outside," he calls to them. "The sun is not dangerous at all. It feels warm and wonderful!"

The other trolls stand there gaping, hardly able to believe their eyes. Why doesn't he crumble to pieces? they murmur to each other. Why isn't he melting in the sun? Because that is the way it is - the way it has always been!

"Look at me," sings out Little Troll. He is dancing across the clearing with all the animals. "You have to take the risk. You have to dare!

"What kind of troll is this child of ours?" cry Mama and Papa.

"Goodness gracious!" says someone else. "Perhaps he isn't a troll at all? There's always been something strange about that child...

But little by little, they get braver. They dare! First one - then another - then many. Until the whole clearing is full of trolls, large and small, standing there squinting in the sunshine - and laughing!

That night a great feast is held in the forest. A feast in honor of Little Troll.

The moose give him a new red tail ribbon.

Mama and Papa are terribly proud.

The Troll King himself holds a speech for him.

"For thousands of years, we trolls have run and hid every time the sun rose!" says the Troll King. "But thanks to Little Troll, we can go out whenever we want to now!

For we know that it is only those who are hard and cold-hearted and bad who will crumble to pieces. Those who think warm thoughts need never fear the sun. And those who have good friends and are themselves a good friend to others need never fear anything in the world!

And from that day on trolls have been about both day and night. For they are like the rest of us. Some are good and some are bad. But no one is so bad that they crumble to pieces!